The Four Grannies

Granny Two stared at Granny One. 'What are *you* doing here?' she said.

'My duty,' said Granny One. 'I've come to look after the children.'

'So have I,' said Granny Two. 'I can manage perfectly.'

'Of course you can't,' said Granny One. 'You fuss all the time, and you spoil the children.'

'And you,' said Granny Two, 'are cruel to them.'

Also in Beaver by Diana Wynne Jones

The Magicians of Caprona
The Time of the Ghost
Power of Three

The Four Grannies

Diana Wynne Jones

Illustrated by Thelma Lambert

Beaver Books

A Beaver Book

Published by Arrow Books Limited
62–5 Chandos Place, London WC2N 4NW
An imprint of Century Hutchinson Ltd
London Melbourne Sydney Auckland Johannesburg
and agencies throughout the world

First published by Hamish Hamilton Ltd 1980
Beaver edition 1981
Reprinted 1983 and 1989

Set in Baskerville

Reproduced, printed and bound in Great Britain by
Hazell Watson & Viney Limited
Member of BPCC plc
Aylesbury, Bucks, England

ISBN 0 09 963890 8

Contents

1 Erg Gets an Idea   7

2 More Grannies Arrive   17

3 Emily Gets Converted   28

4 A Large Yellow Teddy Bear   36

5 How to Keep Four Grannies Busy   44

6 Erg's Invention Works   55

7 Supergranny   66

1

Erg Gets an Idea

Erg's Dad and Emily's Mum found they had to go away to a Conference for four days, leaving Erg and Emily at home.

'I want a house to come back to,' said Erg's Dad, thinking of the time Erg had borrowed the front door to make an underground fort in the garden.

'We'd better ask one of the Grannies to come and look after them,' said Emily's Mum, knowing that if Erg did not borrow a thing, Emily could be trusted to fall over it and break it. Emily was younger than Erg, but she was enormous. She needed bigger shoes than Erg's Dad.

There were four Grannies to choose from, because Erg's Dad and Emily's Mum had both been divorced before they married one another.

Granny One was strict. She wore her hair scraped back from her forbidding

face and her favourite saying was, 'Life is always saying No.' Since Life did not have a voice, Granny One spoke for it, and said No about once every five minutes.

Granny Two was a worrier. She could worry about anything. She was fond of ringing up in the middle of the night to ask if Emily was getting enough vitamins, or – in her special, hushed worrying voice – if Erg ought to be sent to a Special School.

Granny Three was very rich and very stingy. She was the one Emily hated most. Granny Three always arrived with a large box of chocolates. She would give Erg's Dad a chocolate, and Emily's Mum a chocolate, and eat six herself, and take the rest of the box away with her when she went. Erg agreed with Emily that this was mean, but he thought Granny Three was more fun than the others, because she had a new car and different coloured hair every time she came.

Granny Four was a saint. She was gentle and quavery and wrinkled. If Erg and Emily quarrelled in front of her, or even spoke loudly, Granny Four promptly came over faint and had to have a doctor.

Granny Four was the one Erg and Emily chose to look after them. If you could avoid making Granny Four feel faint she usually let you do what you wanted. But, when Emily's Mum rang Granny Four to ask her, Granny Four was faint already. She had been let down over a Save the Children Bazaar and was too ill to come.

So, despite the shrill groans of Erg and the huge moans of Emily, Emily's Mum phoned Granny One. To Erg's relief, Granny One was going on holiday and could not come either. So that left Granny Two, because Granny Three had never been known to look after anyone but herself. But Erg's Dad phoned Granny Three, all the same, hoping she might pay for someone to look after Erg and Emily. Granny Three said she thought it was an excellent idea for Emily and Erg to look after themselves.

Erg's Dad phoned Granny Two. 'What!' exclaimed Granny Two, hushed

and worried. 'Leave dear Erg and poor little Emily all alone, for all that time!'

'But we're only going to Scotland for four days,' Erg's Dad protested.

'I know, dear,' said Granny Two. 'But I'm thinking of *you*. Scotland is covered with oil these days and *so* dangerous!'

Erg and Emily were not looking forward to Granny Two. They waved their parents off gloomily, and sat about waiting for Granny Two to arrive. She was a long time coming. Emily fidgeted round the living-room like an impatient horse, knocking things over right and left. Erg felt an idea coming on. He wandered away to the kitchen to see what he could find.

All the food was wrapped up and carefully labelled so that Granny Two could find it, but Erg found a biscuit-tin. It had holes in the lid from the time he had started a caterpillar farm. Inside were the works of a clock he had once borrowed. It seemed a good beginning for an invention. He collected other things: an egg-beater, the blades off the mixer, a sardine-tin-opener, and a skewer. He

took them all back to the living-room and began fitting them together. The invention was already looking quite promising, when the phone rang. Emily bounced up to answer it, and, quite naturally, she trod on the invention as she went and squashed it flat. Erg roared with rage.

It was Granny Two on the phone. 'I'm terribly sorry, dear. I'd got halfway, when I thought I'd left my kitchen tap on. I'm just setting out again now.'

'*Was* your tap on?' asked Emily.

'No, dear. But just suppose it had been.'

Emily went back to the living-room to find Erg still roaring with rage. 'Look what you've done! You've ruined my invention!'

Emily looked at the invention. It looked like a squashed biscuit-tin with egg-beaters sticking out of it. 'It's only a squashed biscuit-tin,' she said. 'And you ought to put those egg-beaters back.'

But Erg had just discovered that the hand-beater fitted beautifully into a split in the side of the biscuit-tin.

'You're not supposed to have any of them,' said Emily. But Erg took no notice. He wound the handle of the egg-beater. The battered metal of the tin went in and out as if it were breathing, and the pieces of clock inside made a most interesting noise. Emily got annoyed at the way Erg had forgotten her. 'Put those things *back, you horrible little boy!*' she roared.

She was trampling towards Erg to take the invention apart, when a shocked voice said, 'Emily! *Children!*'

They looked round to find Granny
Four in the doorway. She was pale and
quavery and threatening to faint.

2

More Grannies Arrive

Erg and Emily tried to stop Granny Four fainting by smiling politely. 'I thought you weren't coming,' said Erg.

'I couldn't leave you two poor children all alone,' Granny Four said in a failing voice.

Emily and Erg looked at one another. Neither of them had quite the courage to say Granny Two was already on her way.

'Here you are, dear,' Granny Four said to Emily. Shakily, she held out a small, elderly book. 'This will put you in a better frame of mind. It's a beautiful little book about a wicked little girl called Emily. You'll find it charming, dear.'

Emily took the book. It was not the kind of gift you could say thank you for easily. 'I'll take it upstairs to read,' Emily said and thundered away so as not to seem ungrateful.

Erg was hoping heartily that Granny Four had something better for him. But it was not much better. It was a shiny red stick, narrower at one end than the other.

'I think it's a chopstick,' said Granny Four. 'It was in the Bazaar.' She must have seen from Erg's expression that he was not loving the chopstick particularly. She went white and leant against the side of the door. 'You can pretend it's a magic wand, dear,' she said reproachfully.

Erg knew she would faint. He took the chopstick hurriedly and jammed it in one of the holes in his invention. It must have caught in the works of the clock inside the squashed tin, because, when he wound the handle of the egg-beater, the skewer, the sardine-tin-opener and the mixer-blades all began to turn round, grating and clanking as they turned. It was much more interesting now.

Granny Four smothered a slight yawn and began to look healthier. 'We can take such delight in simple things!' she said.

But, just then, a voice shouted 'Coo-ee!' and Granny Two staggered in. She had brought four bags of potatoes, two dozen oranges and a packet of health-food. Granny Four took in the situation and turned faint again. Granny Two took in Granny Four and sprang to her side. 'You shouldn't have come, dear. You look ready to collapse! Come upstairs and lie down and I'll make you a nice cup of tea.' And she led Granny Four away.

Erg was rather pleased. It looked as if the two Grannies could keep one another busy while he got on with his invention. He went into the kitchen again. This time he collected the cutters from the mincer, the handle of the hot tap, the knobs off the

cooker, and the clip that held the bag of the vacuum cleaner together. Most of these things threaded very nicely on to the things stuck into the holes on top of the biscuit-tin. When Erg wound the egg-beater this time, the tap top, the mincer-cutters and the cooker knobs all twiddled round and round, quite beautifully. The works of the clock clanked. The tin breathed in and out. And everything ground and grated just like a real machine.

Erg was trying to find a place for the clip from the vacuum cleaner, when he looked up into the outraged face of Granny One.

Granny One! Erg looked up again unbelievingly. She was really there. She was putting down her neat suitcase in order to fold her arms grimly.

'You're on holiday!' he said.

'I cancelled my holiday,' Granny One said grimly. 'To look after you. Take all those things back to the kitchen at once.'

'But you're on holiday,' Erg argued. 'You can have a holiday from saying No, if you like.'

'Life is always saying No,' said Granny One. 'Take those things back.'

'If Life is always saying No,' Erg argued reasonably, 'it's saying No to me taking them back too.'

But Granny One tapped the floor with her knobby shoe, quite impervious to reason. 'I'm waiting. Do as you're told.'

'Oh, bother you!' said Erg.

That was a mistake. It brought a storm down on Erg's head. It started with 'Don't you speak to me like that!' and ended with Erg sullenly carrying the invention out into the hall to take it to pieces in the kitchen.

The noise fetched Granny Two down the stairs. She stared at Granny One. 'What are *you* doing here?' said Granny Two.

'My duty,' said Granny One. 'I've come to look after the children.'

'So have I,' said Granny Two. 'I can manage perfectly.'

'Of course you can't,' said Granny One. 'You fuss all the time, and you spoil the children.'

'And you,' said Granny Two, 'are cruel to them.'

Granny One had her mouth open to make a blistering reply, when Granny Four tottered down the stairs, faintly wringing her hands. Granny One pointed at her unbelievingly. 'Is *she* here too?'

'Yes, dear, but she can't manage on her own,' said Granny Two.

'Indeed I can!' Granny Four quavered, clinging to the stair-rail.

'It's just as well I came,' Granny One said grimly. 'I see I shall have to look after the lot of you.'

'I do not need looking after!' Grannies Two and Four said in chorus.

By this time it was clear to Erg that three Grannies kept one another even busier than two. Much relieved, he went into the kitchen. There he put the hot tap top back, and the knobs from the cooker, because he knew Granny One would notice those. Then he went out of the back door and into the living-room by the French window and hid the invention safely behind the sofa. Then he went out into the hall again. The Grannies were still insulting one another.

'I didn't know you all hated one another,' he said.

To his surprise, this stopped the argument at once. All the Grannies turned and assured Erg that they loved one another very much. Then they turned and assured one another. After which, they all went into the kitchen for a cup of tea.

Erg went back to work on his invention behind the sofa. The clip off the vacuum cleaner fitted nicely on the end of the sardine-tin-opener. But the invention needed something else to make it perfect. Erg could not think what it needed. He could not think clearly, because the Grannies were now going up and down stairs, calling out about potatoes and rattling at doors.

Finally, Granny Two came into the living-room. 'Erg, dear – Oh dear! He's vanished too. I'm so worried.'

'No I haven't,' Erg said, bobbing up from behind the sofa. 'I'm playing at hiding,' he explained, before Granny Two could ask. 'What's the matter?'

'Emily's locked herself in the bathroom, dear. Be a dear and go and get her out.'

3

Emily Gets Converted

Erg sighed and went upstairs. But it was not a wasted journey. The thought of the bathroom put into his head exactly what would make the invention perfect. It needed glass tubes, with blue water bubbling in them, going *plotterta-plotterta* like inventions did in films. He banged at the bathroom door.

'Go away!' boomed Emily from inside. She sounded tearful. 'I'm busy. I'm reading Granny Four's book.'

'Why are you doing it in there?' Erg asked.

'Because they keep interrupting and asking where to put potatoes and oranges.'

'They want you to come out.'

'I'm not going to,' Emily boomed. 'Not till I've read it. It's beautiful. It's ever so sad.' Erg could hear her sobbing as he went away downstairs.

He went to the kitchen, where the
Grannies were sitting among mounds of
potatoes and oranges, and told them
Emily was reading.

He thought he would never understand
Grannies. One by one, they tiptoed to
the bathroom, rattled the handle and
whispered that there was a cup of tea
outside. 'And don't hurt your eyes, dear,'
Granny Two whispered. 'I'm pushing a
biscuit under the door for you.'

It seemed to be keeping them busy.
Erg sat behind the sofa and got on with

thinking how to make blue water go *plotterta-plotterta*. But he had still not worked it out when Granny Four came and quavered to him that Emily had not touched her tea. Nor had he when Granny Two came to tell him that Emily was ruining her eyes. Nor had he when Granny One came and told him to go out and get some nice fresh air.

Erg was annoyed. He wished he had thought of locking himself in the bathroom too. And he was even more annoyed when Emily at last came out. She came straight to the sofa and crashed heavily down on it with her chin resting on the back.

'What are you making, dear brother?' she said in a sweet cooing voice.

Erg looked up at her suspiciously. There were tear-streaks down Emily's face and an expression on it even more saintly than Granny Four's. 'What's the matter with you?' he said.

Emily turned her eyes piously to the ceiling. 'I have taken a vow to be good, dear brother,' she said. 'It was that beautiful sad book Granny Four gave me.

The girl in it was called Emily too, and she was terribly punished for her wickedness.'

'Go away,' said Erg. He was not sure he could bear it if Emily was going to be a saint as well as Granny Four.

'Ah, dear brother,' cooed Emily, 'do not spurn me. I must stay and pray for you. You have wickedly taken all the kitchen things for that Thing you're making.'

'It's not a Thing!' Erg said angrily. Up till now he had not truly considered what his invention was, but Emily so annoyed him that he said rudely, 'It's a prayer-machine. You wind the handle and it answers your prayer.'

'Sinful boy!' Emily said, with her eyes on the ceiling again. 'Let us pray. I pray that my beloved brother Erchenwald Randolph Gervase turns into a good boy—'

That was the most dreadful insult. Erg lost his temper. Usually when people said his string of terrible names, he hit them, but Emily was so much bigger than he was that he had never yet dared hit her.

Instead, in a frenzy, he wound at the egg-beater. The squashed tin breathed in and out. The works of the clock ground and crunched inside. The chopstick revolved. The skewer twiddled. The sardine-opener and the mincer-cutters wobbled and whirled. Erg wound furiously: *pray pray pray praypraypray*. 'Take Emily away!' he shouted. 'I don't want her!'

In the midst of the noise, he thought he heard Emily stop being a saint and start shouting at him like she usually did. But he did not stop winding. *Pray pray pray praypraypray*.

When at last his arm became too tired to go on, he left off winding and looked up to glare at Emily. She was not there. In her place, with its chin resting on the back of the sofa, was a large yellow teddy bear.

4

A Large Yellow Teddy Bear

Erg stared at the teddy. The bear stared back at him. There was a sorrowful expression in its glass eyes and reproach written all over its yellow furry muzzle.

'Go away,' Erg said to it. 'You're not Emily. You're just pretending.'

But the bear remained, leaning on the back of the sofa, staring reproachfully.

Erg took an alarmed look at his invention. *Could* it be a prayer-machine? Could the chopstick perhaps really be a magic wand? These things just did not happen. On the other hand, he had never seen the teddy before in his life, and its furry face did look remarkably like Emily's. It was big too, about as much too large for a teddy as Emily was for a girl. Erg tried not to think of what the Grannies would say. He got up and searched the living-room. Then he searched the garden.

Emily was nowhere in either. Erg went out into the hall to search the rest of the house.

He stopped short. The front door was wide open. Granny Three was coming in through it lugging bright red suitcases. Granny Three, of all people! Erg stared. Granny Three's hair was pale baby pink this time, and the new car outside in the road was bright snake green.

'There's no need to stare,' Granny Three said to him. 'I've come to look after you. Have you seen Emily?'

'No,' said Erg, trying hard not to look guilty.

'Why not?' said Granny Three. 'I've brought her such a sweet dress.' She put the suitcases down and picked up a dress from the hall stand. Erg blinked. It was a very small dress. It did not look as if it would fit the teddy bear, let alone Emily.

Still, this was the first time Granny Three had ever been known to give any-one anything.

The kitchen door opened and Grannies Four, Two and One looked out to see what was happening.

Granny Three took Granny Four in and, behind her, the unwelcoming faces of Grannies Two and One. She patted her pink hair and drew herself up tall. 'I had to come,' she said. 'My conscience wouldn't let me leave those two poor children alone.'

Erg was interested to hear that Granny Three thought she had a conscience. He always thought he inherited his lack of conscience from Granny Three. He looked at the other Grannies to see what they thought.

Grannies Two and One did indeed draw breath as if they intended to say something thoroughly crushing, but then they looked at Erg and did not say it. Grannies Three and Four looked at Erg too. All four put on sweet smiles.

And Erg felt horrible. He discovered he must have a conscience too. He could not think why else he should feel so guilty about that teddy bear. Granny Three said brightly, 'Well, what can I do? I brought my apron.' Erg crept away from them upstairs and searched the rest of the house. But Emily was not anywhere. And when Erg went downstairs again, the teddy still sat accusingly on the sofa. Erg was forced to believe that he had indeed turned Emily into a teddy bear.

He dared not tell the Grannies. When they called him to lunch, he said, 'Emily's locked in the bathroom again.'

'But she'll miss her dinner,' quavered Granny Four.

Granny Three, who had settled in as if she had always lived there, said, 'Then there'll be more for us. No, dear,' she added to Granny One, 'you must always

mash potatoes with cream. I brought some cream.'

Granny Two could not take the matter so calmly. 'We must get Emily out before she grows up peculiar!' she said, and she set off upstairs to the bathroom.

Erg raced up with her and was just in time to wedge the landing carpet under the door so that it would not open. He left Granny Two there rattling and calling and raced down to the living-room. The teddy still sat there, vast and yellow, on the sofa. But Erg felt it would be just like

Emily to turn into something else while he was not looking. Then he might not be able to find her to turn her back. He decided to take the teddy in to lunch with him. That was terrible. Granny Three actually smiled kindly. Granny Four took the teddy and sat it in a chair of its own. 'Is it a teddy-weddy then?' she said, and pretended to feed the teddy with mashed potato. Granny One kept looking from Erg to the teddy to Granny Four and snorting sarcastically. And when Granny Two came downstairs, she said, 'Oh, the fairies have brought you a teddy! How exciting!'

In between all this, all the Grannies wondered where Emily was and said she was growing up peculiar.

But halfway through lunch, Erg noticed the glass salt-cellar, and he saw the way out of his troubles. Let him put that salt-cellar upside down, with a drinking-straw in it. Let both be filled with blue water going *plotterta-plotterta*. And Erg knew the machine would answer his prayer and turn the teddy back into Emily again. The trouble was, could he do it before the Grannies noticed that the teddy's reproachful face was exactly like Emily's?

Erg knew that he was going to have to keep all four Grannies very busy.

5

How to Keep
Four Grannies Busy

When lunch was over, the Grannies all put on aprons to wash up. Erg said he would take some lunch to Emily. Granny One sternly handed him two oranges.

'Eat those for vitamins,' she said.

'That's right, dear,' agreed Granny Two. 'Push Emily's under the door for her.'

Erg went upstairs and parked the teddy and the lunch in the bath. Then he wedged the door again and went down to the living-room. He peeled both oranges and broke the peel into very small bits, which he scattered all over the carpet. But it takes a lot to keep four Grannies busy. Erg was still gulping and feeling much too full of orange, when Granny One escaped from the washing up and stood in the doorway staring grimly at the bits of orange peel.

'I'll use the vacuum cleaner on it, shall I?' Erg said brightly.

'No you will not,' said Granny One. She went and got the vacuum cleaner herself and firmly plugged it in.

Erg watched expectantly as she switched it on. Since the clip that held the bag together was now part of the prayer-machine, there was nothing to hold the dust in the cleaner at all. Dust came out in a cloud, like an explosion. Big wads of dirt followed it. And after that came orange peel, whirling and whizzing. Granny One switched the cleaner off in a hurry and screamed for help.

Granny Four hurried in and turned faint in the dust. Granny Three came and turned the vacuum cleaner upside down. All the rest of the dust fell out of it.

'I don't understand these things,' Granny Three said fretfully. 'Telephone for a man.'

'Pull out the plug first!' gasped Granny Two, hastening to the scene. 'There's electricity leaking into it all the time!'

'Nonsense!' snapped Granny One, coming to her senses. 'Erg, what have you done to this machine?'

But Erg was already tip-toeing into the kitchen. Hastily, he unscrewed the salt-cellar and poured the salt into the nearest thing – which happened to be the sugar bowl. He snatched up a packet of transparent drinking-straws. Finally, he turned the tap on over the half-finished washing up. It was not long before bubbly water was pouring over on to the floor. Erg turned the tap off again.

'Hey!' he yelled. 'You left the tap running!'

This fetched all four Grannies back at a gallop.

Satisfied, Erg went back into the dust-hung living-room and collected the invention from behind the sofa. He took it up to the bathroom and locked himself in with it and the salt-cellar and the straws and the teddy and Emily's lunch. He thought he had given himself an hour's peace at least.

But it takes more than dust and water

to keep four Grannies busy. Ten minutes later, Granny Four was rattling at the bathroom door. 'Emily, dear, are you all right?'

'It's me in here now,' Erg called. 'Emily's gone for a walk.'

'Then could you let me in, dear?' Granny Four called back. 'I'd like a little wash before I go for my rest.'

'You can't *rest!*' Erg called. He was horrified. Next thing he knew, they would all be up here, fussing about with cups of tea and hot-water-bottles and things.

'Why not, dear?' quavered Granny Four.

Erg cast about for a reason. His eye fell on the washing-basket. 'There's all the washing to do,' he shouted. 'I'll bring it downstairs for you, shall I?'

'I'd better go and tell them,' quavered Granny Four and tottered away.

But, when Erg looked in the washing-basket, it was empty. Nothing daunted, Erg took off the clothes he was wearing and put them in the basket. Grannies always said clothes were dirty when you

had hardly worn them anyway. Then he went to Emily's room and his own and collected all the clothes he could find there. Erg unfolded them and scrunched them up in his hands and rammed them into the basket. Then he put on clean clothes and staggered downstairs with the basket.

'Here you are,' he said, emptying the crumpled heap on the kitchen floor.

The four Grannies were gathered there eating chocolates out of the box Granny Three had brought. They gave the heap various looks of suffering and dismay. Granny Four turned pale. Granny Two sprang up saying she would fill the sink with nice hot water.

'You're allowed to use the washing-machine,' Erg said.

'Oh no, dear,' said Granny Two. 'Electricity doesn't mix with water. It gets into the clothes, you know.'

On reflection, Erg thought that washing in the sink would keep them busier. He took the basket back to the bathroom. Then he undid the toilet cistern and took out the blue block in it to make the blue water that was to go *plotterta-plotterta*. Then he thought he had better check to see how busy the Grannies were.

He peeped round the kitchen door to find them quite out of control again. Granny Three was standing in the heap of clothes sorting them out. She took up a shirt, shook it fiercely, and passed it to Granny One. 'This is clean too,' she said. 'I think someone has been making work for us.'

'Quite right,' said Granny One, holding the shirt up to the light. 'Clean *and* ironed.' She passed the shirt to Granny Two, who smoothed it out and folded it carefully and passed it to Granny Four. Granny Four turned to put the shirt on a large heap of others and saw Erg watching.

'Will you take these back upstairs, dear,' she said.

'All right,' said Erg. 'And then I'll

bring down the rest of the washing, shall I?'

'*Is* there more?' Granny Three asked, transferring her angry look from the next shirt to Erg.

'Oh yes,' said Erg. There was going to be, if it killed him.

He went upstairs with the pile of clothes and locked himself in the bathroom again. At least, Erg thought, he had kept the Grannies too busy to think of Emily for some time. But, at the rate they were going, they would be asking about her any minute now.

Erg took the plate of lunch out of the bath and used it to dirty ten of the shirts in the pile. But, though he spread the lunch very thinly and carefully with his toothbrush, it would not go round more than ten shirts. He found himself looking longingly at his invention where it sat in the wash-basin. Even without the blue water, it had already worked quite well. Erg decided to give it another try.

He wound the egg-beater – *pray pray pray praypraypray*. The tin crunched in and out. The mixer-blades, the skewer and the sardine-opener grated and revolved. The vacuum cleaner clip, the mincer-cutters and the chopstick wobbled and twirled. 'Make the washing keep them busy,' Erg said, winding away.

6

Erg's Invention Works

Erg's clean clothes had become quite well covered with lunch and the blue from the toilet-block. He took them off and put them in the basket with the ten shirts. In their place, he put on the first clothes left in the heap: Emily's nightdress, his own jeans and Emily's school shirt. Dressed in this flowing raiment, he went down to the living-room to roll in the dust there. But Granny Four was there, feebly flicking with a duster.

'What are you doing, dear?'

'Playing oil-sheiks,' said Erg. He went out into the garden and rolled in a flower-bed.

Granny Four was not in the living-room when he came back. To Erg's horror, she met him outside the bathroom, carrying the teddy. 'You forgot teddy-weddy, dear.'

It was awful how the Grannies kept getting out of control. Erg locked the door and took off the raiment. He put on the next things: Emily's tartan skirt and a frilly blouse. This time, he took the teddy with him and wedged the bathroom door shut.

'What are you doing now, dear?' asked Granny Four.

'Playing North Sea oil,' Erg explained. 'The teddy is my sporran.' He went and rolled in the flower-bed again.

This time, he got safely back to the bathroom. But he did not dare leave the teddy behind when he set out again in the next set of clothes, which were his own striped pyjamas.

'I'm playing going to bed,' he told Granny Four before she could ask, and went and rolled in the flower-bed once more.

While he was rolling, Granny Two and Granny Three came into the garden with a basket of washing to hang on to the clothes-line. They were struggling to hold a ballooning skirt and a kicking pair of jeans in what seemed a very strong wind. Erg lay in the earth and watched. The skirt made a strong dive and almost got away. Both Grannies caught it. It took them some time to get it pegged, and the dress they took up next seemed to be blowing even harder. Erg licked one finger and thoughtfully held it up. There was almost no wind. Yet the row of things on the line were flapping and struggling and kicking as if there was half a gale.

Interesting. But where was Granny One? Erg got up and went through the back door into the kitchen to check on Granny One. She was not there. But while Erg was looking round to make sure, the pile of wet washing on the draining board rolled heavily over and went *flap*, down on to the kitchen floor. Erg could see it oozing and trickling and spreading over the floor. He watched with interest. The washing was definitely working its way over towards the nearest heap of potatoes to get itself nice and dirty again.

Erg was delighted. The prayer-machine worked! He went upstairs in his earthy pyjamas, convinced that the chopstick really must be some kind of magic wand. He only needed to get the blue water working, and he could turn Emily back again.

But Granny One was outside the bathroom door, knocking and rattling at it. She turned and looked at Erg. He had rarely seen her look so grim.

'Take those pyjamas off at *once!* What are you and Emily—?'

'The washing,' Erg said hastily, 'has fallen on the kitchen floor.'

To his relief, Granny One pushed past him and went rushing downstairs to rescue the washing. Erg locked himself in the bathroom again and put the teddy back in the bath. He was beginning to feel that four Grannies were too much for any boy to control. There was another annoying thing, too. There were no more of his own clothes left to wear. He had got them all dirty. He stayed in his pyjamas and got down to work on the salt-cellar at last.

He had the salt-cellar nicely filled with blue water, when he was interrupted again, by quivering shouts from the garden. Erg could not resist opening the bathroom window to look. There was washing all over the garden. Some of it was blowing and kicking in the gooseberry bushes. The rest of it was whirling round and round the lawn with all four Grannies chasing it. Satisfied, Erg shut the window. He was determined to finish his invention.

It was much trickier than he had thought. The hole in the lid of the salt-cellar was not big enough to get a straw through. Erg had to enlarge it with the skewer. And when he had got the straw to go through, he could not get the salt-cellar to stand properly upside-down on top of the machine. He had to bend open the blades of the electric mixer to hold it. And when he had done that, he still could not get the blue water to go *plotterta-plotterta*. It simply ran down through the straw and into the inside of the biscuit-tin. When Erg wound the handle of the egg-beater, the water came out of the holes in the tin in blue showers.

'Bother!' said Erg.

As he put more blue water into the salt-cellar, he began to feel that every-thing was getting out of hand. The machine would not work. The earthy front of his pyjamas was blue and soaking, and so was most of the bathroom. And, to crown it all, there was a new outcry from the Grannies, from the kitchen this time. This was followed by feet on the stairs.

Next moment, all four Grannies were outside the bathroom door.

'Come out of there at once!' snapped Granny One.

'We're so worried, dear,' hushed Granny Two.

'It was very unkind of you, dear,' quavered Granny Four, 'to fill the sugar bowl with salt.'

But it was Granny Three who really alarmed Erg. 'You know,' she said, 'that child has done something with Emily. I've not set eyes on her all the time I've been here.'

Erg's eyes went guiltily to the sad face of the teddy in the bath.

Outside the door, Granny Two said, 'I shall phone the Fire Brigade to get him out.'

'And spank him when he is,' Granny One agreed.

Erg listened to no more. He rammed the salt-cellar and the straw back in place and wound the egg-beater. *Pray pray pray praypraypray*. Blue water squirted. The works of the clock sploshed. Round and round went the chopstick, the mixer-blades, the salt-cellar, the skewer, the sardine-opener, the mincer-cutters, the straw and the clip off the vacuum cleaner.

'Only one Granny,' prayed Erg, winding desperately. 'I can't manage more than one – please!'

7

Supergranny

There was a sudden silence outside the bathroom door. It's worked! Erg thought.

'Erg,' said a large quavery voice outside. 'Erg, open this door.'

'In a minute,' Erg called.

The words were hardly out of his mouth when the bathroom door leapt, and crashed open against the wall. The one Granny Erg had asked for came in. Only one. But Erg stared at her in horror. She was two metres tall and huge all over. Her hair was the baby pink of Granny Three's. Her face was the stern face of Granny One, except that it wore the worried look of Granny Two. Her voice was the quavery voice of Granny Four, but it was four times as loud. Erg knew at a glance that what he had here was all four Grannies in one. They had blended into Supergranny. He jumped up to run.

Supergranny swept towards Erg. With one hand she caught Erg's arm in a grip of steel. At the same time, she was keenly scanning the rest of the bathroom.

'What is this mess?' she quavered menacingly. 'And where is Emily?'

Erg dared not tell the truth. He avoided the teddy's accusing stare. 'Emily went to play in the park,' he said.

'Very well,' said Supergranny. 'We shall go and get her. Come along, dear.'

'I can't go like this!' Erg protested, looking down at his earthy, blue, wet pyjamas.

All the Grannies were a little deaf when it suited them. Supergranny was super-deaf. 'Come along, dear,' she said. She plucked the teddy out of the bath and planted it in Erg's arms. 'Don't forget teddy-weddy the fairies brought you.' And she pulled Erg towards the door.

All Erg could think of was to spare one hand from the teddy and snatch up his invention from the wash-basin as he was pulled away. Blue water from it trickled down his legs as Supergranny towed him downstairs, but Erg hung on to it grimly.

As soon as he got a chance, he was going to wind the egg-beater again and get Supergranny sent to Mars – which was surely where she belonged.

But, in the hall, Supergranny's piercing eye fell on the prayer-machine. 'You can't take that nasty thing, dear,' she said. She dragged it away from Erg and dropped it on the floor. Miserably, Erg tried dropping the teddy too. But Supergranny picked it up again and once more planted it in Erg's arms. 'Come along, dear.'

Erg found himself in the street outside the house, in wet blue pyjamas, with one hand clutching a huge teddy and the other in the iron grip of Supergranny. Behind him, the front door crashed shut. Erg could tell by the noise that it had locked itself. 'Have you got a key?' he said hopelessly.

All the Grannies were a little vague at times, when it suited them. Supergranny was super-vague. 'I don't know, dear. Come along.'

Erg knew he was locked out of the house and the prayer-machine locked in.

As a last hope, he tried lingering beside Granny Three's snake green car. 'Can we drive to the park?'

But three of the Grannies did not know how to drive, and that cancelled out the one who did. 'I don't know how to drive, dear,' said Supergranny.

So Erg was forced to trot along the pavement beside Supergranny. They kept passing people Erg knew. Not one of these people spared a glance for Supergranny. It was as if they saw pink-haired super-women every day. But every single person stared at Erg, and Erg's pyjamas, and the huge teddy-bear. Erg tried to keep an expression on his face of a boy playing woad-stained Ancient British convicts, who had just slain a fierce teddy-bear. But, either that was too hard an idea for one face to express, or Erg did not express it very well. Almost everybody laughed.

Erg was glad when they reached the park and found it nearly empty, except for some girls on the swings.

Here, Supergranny seemed to forget they had come to look for Emily. But that did not help Erg. Supergranny led him over to the slide and the swings. 'You play, dear. Slide down the slide, while I rest my poor feet.' She sat heavily on the nearest park bench.

Erg tried to defy her. 'What if I don't slide down the slide?' he asked.

'Awful things happen to little boys who disobey,' Supergranny quavered placidly.

Erg looked her in the steely eye and believed it. He leant the teddy against the steps of the slide and began bitterly to climb up. He knew that when he got to the top, the girls on the swings would see him and laugh too.

But when he got to the top of the slide, everyone had left the swings except one big girl. She was such a big girl that she had to swing with her legs stuck straight out in front of her. Erg sat at the top of the slide and stared.

That big girl was Emily!

Unbelievingly, Erg craned to look over his shoulder. The big yellow teddy-bear was still leaning against the steps of the slide. Had the invention perhaps not been a prayer-machine after all? Erg looked hopefully over at the park bench. Supergranny still sat there. Her pink head was nodding in a super-doze.

Erg flung himself on the slide and shot down it. He shot off the bottom and raced across to the swings.

'Emily!' he panted. 'What happened? Where did you go?'

Emily gave Erg an unfriendly look. 'To have lunch with my friend Josephine,' she said. 'Dear brother,' she added, and stood up against the swing ready to shoot forward on it and kick Erg in the stomach.

'Oh, be nice, please!' Erg begged her. '*Why* did you go?'

'Because you were so horrid to me,' said Emily. 'And then when I opened the front door, Granny Three was outside heaving a teddy out of her car, and I couldn't face her. I hate Granny Three. So I hid behind the door while she went to give you the teddy, and then I ran round to Josephine's.'

So the teddy had come from Granny Three. It was all a terrible mistake. It

was a natural mistake, perhaps, because Granny Three had never been known to give anyone anything before, but a mistake all the same. And to make matters worse, Supergranny had noticed Erg was not sliding. She sprang up and came scouring across to the swings, calling for Erg in a long quavering hoot, like a magnified owl. It was such a noise, that people were running from the other end of the park to see what was the matter.

Erg watched her coming, feeling like a drowning man whose life is passing before him in a flash. The prayer-machine had been working all along, he knew now. He had not asked it to turn Emily into a teddy bear, but he *had* asked it to send her away, and it did. It had not needed blue water. It had made the washing keep the Grannies busy without. It did not even need to be a machine. It was the chopstick that did things. And, like all such things, Erg saw wretchedly, as Supergranny pounded towards him, it gave you three wishes, and he had used all three. He had no way of getting rid of Supergranny at all.

Emily stared at the vast, running Supergranny. 'Whoever is that!'

'Supergranny,' said Erg. 'She's all of them, and she's after me. Please help me. I'll never be horrible to you again.'

'Don't make promises you can't keep,' said Emily, but she let go of the swing and stood up.

Supergranny pounded up. '*There* you are, Emily!' she hooted. 'I've been *so* worried!'

'I was only in the park,' Emily said. 'I think we'll go home now.' She was, Erg was interested to see, nearly as large as Supergranny.

'Yes, dear,' Supergranny said, almost meekly. And when Emily picked up the teddy and gave it to her, Supergranny took it without complaining.

They set off home. 'How are we going to get in?' Erg whispered to Emily. 'She's locked us out.'

'No problem. I took the key,' Emily said.

Halfway home, Supergranny's feet began super-killing her. She came over super-faint and had to lean on Erg and

Emily. Erg had to stand staggering under her huge weight on his own while Emily fetched out her key and opened the front door.

'Good Lord!' said Emily.

The hall was full of dirty clothes. Dry dirty clothes were now galloping and billowing downstairs. Wet dirty clothes were crawling soggily through from the kitchen. Emily shot a horrified look at Supergranny and went charging indoors to catch the nearest pair of dirty jeans. She tripped over the invention in the middle of the floor. She fell flat on her face. *Crunch. Crack*. The egg-beater rolled out from one side in two pieces. The chopstick rolled the other way, *snapped in half*.

'*Ow!*' said Emily.

The clothes flopped down and lay where they fell. Supergranny's mighty arm seemed to disentangle itself between Erg's hands. It was suddenly four arms. Erg let go, and found himself surrounded by the four Grannies, all staring into the hall too.

'Get up, Emily!' snapped Granny One.

'Oh, Erg!' said Granny Two. 'Out of doors in pyjamas! You *are* growing up peculiar!'

'I shall take your teddy away again,' said Granny Three. 'Look at this mess! You don't deserve nice toys!'

'Let's have a nice cup of tea,' quavered

Granny Four. A thought struck her. She turned pale. 'We can do without sugar,' she said faintly. 'It's better for us.'

Erg looked from one to the other. He was very relieved, and very grateful to Emily. But he knew he was not going to enjoy the next three days.

BEAVER BOOKS FOR YOUNGER READERS

Have you heard about all the exciting stories available in Beaver? You can buy them in bookstores or they can be ordered directly from us. Just complete the form below and send the right amount of money and the books will be sent to you at home.

☐ THE BIRTHDAY KITTEN	Enid Blyton	£1.50
☐ THE WISHING CHAIR AGAIN	Enid Blyton	£1.99
☐ BEWITCHED BY THE BRAIN SHARPENERS	Philip Curtis	£1.75
☐ SOMETHING NEW FOR A BEAR TO DO	Shirley Isherwood	£1.95
☐ REBECCA'S WORLD	Terry Nation	£1.99
☐ CONRAD	Christine Nostlinger	£1.50
☐ FENELLA FANG	Ritchie Perry	£1.95
☐ MRS PEPPERPOT'S OUTING	Alf Prøysen	£1.99
☐ THE WORST KIDS IN THE WORLD	Barbara Robinson	£1.75
☐ THE MIDNIGHT KITTENS	Dodie Smith	£1.75
☐ ONE GREEN BOTTLE	Hazel Townson	£1.50
☐ THE VANISHING GRAN	Hazel Townson	£1.50
☐ THE GINGERBREAD MAN	Elizabeth Walker	£1.50
☐ BOGWOPPIT	Ursula Moray Williams	£1.95

If you would like to order books, please send this form, and the money due to:
ARROW BOOKS, BOOKSERVICE BY POST, PO BOX 29, DOUGLAS, ISLE OF MAN, BRITISH ISLES. Please enclose a cheque or postal order made out to Arrow Books Ltd for the amount due including 22p per book for postage and packing both for orders within the UK and for overseas orders.

NAME ....

ADDRESS ....

....

Please print clearly.

Whilst every effort is made to keep prices low it is sometimes necessary to increase cover prices at short notice. Arrow Books reserve the right to show new retail prices on covers which may differ from those previously advertised in the text or elsewhere.